Beauty and the Beast

Beauty and

the Beast

Retold by Sir Arthur Quiller-Couch

Illustrated by Edmund Dulac

Gramercy Books
New York • Avenel, New Jersey

This 1991 edition is published by Gramercy Books,
distributed by Outlet Book Company, Inc.,
a Random House Company,
40 Engelhard Avenue,
Avenel, New Jersey 07001.

Designed by Melissa Ring

Manufactured in Singapore

ISBN 0-517-06630-0

8 7 6 5 4 3 2

Introduction

Beauty and the Beast is a tale of love and transformation, where dreams and desires are illuminated as if by candlelight in the fragrant garden of a sumptuous palace. It is a tale destined to be told again and again in many different voices.

The pleasure of telling and retelling stories falls not only to the reader, but also to the writer, and, like the story itself, the history of *Beauty and the Beast* is also one of transformation. The fairy tale which has come to be known as *Beauty and the Beast* was first published in English in 1757. It was translated from a work entitled "La Belle et la Bête" by the French children's author, Mme. de Beaumont. According to the *Oxford Companion to Children's Literature*, Mme. de Beaumont's primary source was a 362-page story in Villeneuve's *Contes marins*, "a collection of tales supposedly told by an old woman during a long sea-voyage." *Contes marins* was published in 1740, yet tales of transformation, human and otherwise, go back to ancient literature. Elements of *Beauty and the Beast* also bear a strong resemblance to the story of Cupid and Psyche in Apuleius' *The Golden Ass*, which was written in the second century A.D. Whatever its true origins, *Beauty and the Beast* was an immediate success in England. The story quickly found a place in literature and folklore. Many different versions appeared, even one set in rhymed couplets.

The version of *Beauty and the Beast* presented in this delightful edition comes from the pen of Sir Arthur Thomas Quiller-Couch (1863–1944). Known in the literary circles of his time as the pseudonymous writer "Q," he was a novelist, scholar, poet, parodist, and critic who was also considered to be a master of the short story. His considerable literary skills are reflected in the consummate elegance and simplicity with which he retold this classic fairy tale.

Quiller-Couch's *Beauty and the Beast* was originally published in the early twentieth century in a lavishly illustrated collection of his fairy tales. The illustrator was Edmund Dulac (1882–1953), a French-born artist who became a British subject and was well-known for his imaginative book illustrations. Dulac was a meticulous craftsman, and his illustrations are carefully planned compositions, much like jeweled miniatures. His art is remarkable, but even more astonishing is the intensity of his absorption with the story, which, translated into illustration, transcends ordinary vision. Here is a stage upon which the imagination can act, complete with beautiful scenery to swell the voice of the story.

We are almost at the moment when we can hear the words "Once upon a time. . . ." The book rests comfortably in our hands; the pages stretch out before us, filled with enchantments. Suddenly we can hear a rush of breath, and the heavy padding of feet coming through distant rooms. The beast is here, we can begin.

LOIS HILL

New York
1991

Once upon a time, in a country a long way from here, there stood a flourishing city, full of commerce. And in that city lived a merchant so lucky in all his ventures that it seemed as if fortune waited on his wishes. But although he was enormously rich, he was a widower and had a very large family of six sons and six daughters. Not one of them was yet settled in life. The boys were too young to go out in the world, and the girls, who had everything at home the heart could desire, were in no hurry to risk a change by choosing husbands, although many rich and noble suitors paid court to them.

But one day an unexpected disaster brought this pleasant state of things to an end. Their house caught fire and was burned to the ground. With it perished not only the magnificent furniture, but the merchant's account books, bank notes, gold and silver, and the precious wares on which his wealth depended. Scarcely anything was saved.

This was but the beginning of their misfortunes. The merchant, who up to now had prospered in everything he touched, lost, in a very short while, every ship he had upon the sea. Some were wrecked, others captured by pirates. His agents failed. His clerks in foreign countries proved unfaithful. In short, from the height of riches he suddenly fell into the direst poverty.

Nothing was left to him but one poor little country cottage, at least a hundred leagues from the city in which he had lived. In this cottage he was driven to find refuge, and there he took his family, who were in despair. The daughters especially could not endure the thought of dwelling in such a den (as they called it). At first they had felt sure that on hearing the news their suitors would be tripping one another up in haste to renew their offers of marriage. But in this they were soon undeceived. Their downfall was no sooner known than all these flattering wooers took to their feet in a troop. They fared no better with their intimate friends, who at once dropped them. Nay, those to whom the merchant had formerly shown the greatest kindness were now the most eager to speak ill of him.

So nothing was left for this hapless family but to depart from the city and shut themselves up in the cottage, which stood in the depths of a dismal and almost trackless forest. There were no servants now to wait on them. The sons tilled the ground and swept out the farm sheds. The daughters, dressed like country girls in coarse linen frocks, were forced to turn their delicate hands to the roughest work and live on simple fare of which there was little enough.

Only the youngest daughter showed a brave heart. She had been as despondent as any of them to begin with, but after weeping—as well she might—for her father's misfortunes, she recovered her natural gaiety, made the best of things, tried to forget how ungrateful the world had been, kept her father and her brothers amused with her cheerful wit, and after she had done her work, would sing and play.

Her sisters would not join with her in making the best of things. "It is very easy for you to be happy," the eldest grumbled. "You have low tastes and were born for this kind of life." The fact is, they were all jealous of her because of her sweet temper and good looks. So beautiful, indeed, was this youngest sister that in the old days everyone had agreed to call her Beauty. By that and by no other name she was known. Alone of them she might easily, in the first days of their ruin, have found a husband, but she could not think of this while she could be of use to help and console her family.

*T*wo years passed and then there came news which seemed to offer a hope of escape. One of their father's ships, long supposed to be lost, had arrived in port with a rich cargo. The message further advised his return to the city with speed, or his agents might sell the goods too cheaply and he would lose his gains. So, while his children danced with joy at the news, the merchant set about preparing for his long journey.

In their happiness his daughters loaded him with commissions for gowns and jewels it would have taken a fortune to buy. Only Beauty would not ask for anything. Her father, noting her silence, interrupted the others who still kept adding to their lists of requirements.

"Well, Beauty," he said, "and what shall I bring home for you? Surely you, too, wish for something."

"Dear Father," she answered, "I wish for the most precious thing in the world. That is to see you home again safe and sound."

This answer covered the sisters with confusion, and vexed them so that one of them, speaking up for the others, said tartly, "This small miss is putting on airs. She thinks, no doubt, she cuts a figure with her affected fine sentiments!"

Her father, however, was touched by her good feeling. Nevertheless, he told her to choose something. "For," said he, "at your age it is only natural to like dresses and pretty presents."

"Well, dear Father," she said, "since you insist, I will beg you to bring me home a rose. I have not seen one since we came to live here, and I love roses." In this way Beauty contrived to obey her father and yet to put him to no expense.

The day came for the merchant to embrace them all and bid them farewell. He made his way to the great city, and arrived there to be met with a great disappointment. To be sure his vessel had come safely to port, but his partners, believing him dead, had taken possession of it and divided the cargo between them. To make good his claim he was forced to bring a number of tedious lawsuits. He won them in the end, but only to find, after six months of trouble and expense, that he was almost as poor as when he started.

To make his misery complete, he was forced to travel back in the winter, in the most inclement weather. By the time he reached the outskirts of the forest he was ready to drop with fatigue. But reminding himself that his home was now not many leagues away, he called up what strength remained to him.

As he pushed on through the forest, night overtook him. In the piercing cold, half buried— his horse and he—in the deep snow that hid every pathway, the poor merchant feared that his last hour had come. Not so much as a hut did he pass. The only shelter to be found was the trunk of a hollow tree. And there he cowered through the long night, kept awake by his hunger and the howling of the wolves. Nor did the day bring him much comfort, for thick snow lay everywhere, and not a path was to be seen. It was only after a weary search that he managed to find his horse, who had wandered away and partly sheltered itself in another hollow tree. He mounted and in a little while discovered a sort of track which presently grew easier.

Following this, he found himself in an avenue of trees, at the entrance of which he halted and rubbed his eyes. For no snow had fallen in this avenue, and the trees were tall orange trees, planted in four rows and covered with flowers and fruit. Here and there among the trees were statues, some of single figures, others of groups representing scenes of war, but all colored like real life. At the end of the avenue, straight in front of him, rose a magnificent castle in many terraces.

The merchant rode around to the stable courtyard, which he found empty. There, with half-frozen hands, he unbridled and stabled his horse. Within the doorway he found a staircase of agate with balusters of carved gold. He mounted it and passed through room after room, each more splendidly furnished than the last. They were deliciously warm, too, and he began to feel his limbs again. But he was hungry. Where could he find someone to give him food? Everywhere was silence. And yet the place had no look of being abandoned. Drawing rooms, bed chambers, galleries—all stood unlocked. At last, tired of roaming, he came to a halt in an apartment where someone had lit a bright fire. A sofa drawn up cozily beside it, invited him to sit and warm his limbs. Resting there, he closed his eyes and fell into a deep and grateful slumber.

As weariness had sent him to sleep, so hunger awoke him. He opened his eyes and saw at his elbow a table with meats and wine upon it. He had not eaten for more than twenty-four hours, and lost no time in falling to. He hoped that he might soon have sight of this most gracious host, whoever he might be, and an opportunity of thanking him. Still no one appeared, and now this good food did for him what fatigue had done before. He dropped off again into an easy slumber which lasted for almost four hours. Again awakening, he saw at his elbow another small table—of porphyry this time—upon which the unknown hands had set out a dainty meal of cakes, crystallized fruits, and liqueurs. To

this, too, he did justice. But, as the time still passed and no one appeared, he began to feel terrified, and resolved to search once more through all the rooms. But still he found no one.

He was standing lost in thought, when all of a sudden it came into his mind that some kindly power had perhaps prepared this palace of wonder for him, that it, with all its riches, might indeed be his. Possessed by this notion he once again made a tour of the rooms and took stock of their treasures, planning in his mind how he would divide them among his children, assigning this apartment to one and that to another, and whispering to himself what joy he would carry home after all from his journey. Then he went down into the garden, where—though it was the depth of winter—the birds were singing and the air breathed the scent of a thousand flowers.

"Surely," he told himself, "my daughters will be happy here and never desire any more to go back to the city. Quick! Let me saddle my horse at once and ride home with the news!"

The way to the stable was an alley fenced on either hand with palings, and over the palings hung great clusters of roses in bloom. They reminded him of his promise to Beauty. He plucked one, and was about to pluck a whole nosegay, when he was startled by a horrible noise behind him, and attempted to turn. But behind him stood a hideous beast who was overtaking him and reaching out toward him.

"Who gave you leave to pluck my roses?" roared this monster. "Was it not enough that I made you welcome in my palace and treated you kindly? And you show your gratitude by stealing my flowers! But your insolence shall not go unpunished!"

The good merchant, terrified no less by the sight of this beast than by his threats, dropped the rose and fell to his knees.

"My Lord," he cried, "have pity on me! I am not ungrateful, but after all your kindness I could not guess that so small a thing would offend you."

This speech did not at all abate the beast's wrath. "Hold your tongue, sir," he commanded, "if you can offer me nothing but flatteries and false titles. I am not 'my lord.' I am the beast, and your words will not save you from the death you deserve."

The merchant, although in fear of his life, plucked up courage to tell the monster that the rose which he had been bold to pick was for one of his daughters, by name Beauty. Then, in hope either to delay the beast's vengeance or to touch his compassion, he launched into the tale of all his misfortunes, and of his reasons for the journey, not forgetting to mention Beauty again and her request.

The beast considered for a moment before

answering him in a somewhat milder tone, "I will forgive you, but only on condition that you give me one of your daughters. Someone must make amends for this trespass."

"Heaven forgive me," the merchant entreated, "but how can I promise such a thing? Even were I cruel enough to purchase my life at the cost of a child, on what excuse could I bring her?"

"No excuse is necessary," replied the beast shortly. "Whichever daughter you bring must come here of her own free will, or not at all. Go home and see if there be one brave and loving enough to sacrifice herself to save your life. You seem to be an honest man. Give me your word to return here at the end of a month and bring whichever of your daughters you can persuade to come with you. If you can persuade none of them, you must come alone. And I warn you that, if you fail, I shall come and fetch you."

What was the poor man to do? He promised, for he saw death staring him in the face, and having given his promise he hoped to be allowed to depart. But the beast informed him that he could not go until the next day.

"Then," said he, "at daybreak you will find a horse ready for you who will carry you home in less than no time. Now go and eat your supper, and await my commands."

The merchant, more dead than alive, crept

back to his rooms. There, before a blazing fire, he found a delicious supper spread, inviting him to eat. But so distraught was he, that no food, however delicious, could have tempted him had he not been afraid that the beast might be hiding somewhere to watch him. In fear of this he forced himself to sit and taste of the dishes.

A loud noise in the next room warned him that the beast was coming. Since he could not escape, he mustered what courage he could to conceal his terror, and faced about to the doorway.

"Have you made a good supper?" was the beast's first question.

The merchant in humblest voice answered that, thanks to his host's kind attention, he had fared extremely well.

"I am paying you a visit," said the beast, "to warn you again to be honest with your daughter. Describe me to her just as I am. Let her be free to choose whether she will come or not. But tell her that, her course once chosen, there can be no retreat, or even reflection after you have brought her to me. To break faith then will avail nothing: she will but destroy you without winning her own release."

Again the spirit-broken merchant repeated his promise.

The beast appeared to be content at last. "Retire to bed now," he commanded, "and do not get up tomorrow until you see the sun and hear a golden bell rung. Then, before starting, you will find breakfast laid for you here. Your horse will be standing ready saddled in the courtyard, and you may carry back the rose to your daughter Beauty— as you call her. For the rest, I count on seeing you back in a month's time. So, farewell."

The merchant, who dared not disobey a single one of these orders, retired to bed at once, though without any temptation to sleep. And again, though he passed a wretched night, he was punctual to rise with the sun. A golden bell rang, and prompt on the sound he found breakfast laid, still by unseen hands. After breakfast he went down to the stables, and on his way paused to pick up the rose, which lay in the alley where it had dropped from his hand. It was as fresh as ever, and smelled as sweetly as though it still grew on the tree.

A few paces further on he found his horse standing ready saddled, with a handsome cloak of furs, far warmer than his own, lying across the saddle. He put it on and mounted, and now he had to wonder at yet another miracle. His horse set off at an incredible speed, so that before he could even turn in the saddle the palace had disappeared from sight.

Could the horse have felt the weight on the good man's mind, it would have never made such a pace. But it took its own way, insensible to the rein, and did not halt until it reached the cottage.

The merchant's sons and daughters had rushed out at his approach, although it was not until he drew quite close that they recognized their father in this horseman superbly cloaked, with a rose at his holster, and mounted on a horse that traveled at such a speed. When they recognized him, they were sure that he brought the best of news. But the tears that trickled down his cheeks as he dismounted told them another story.

His first move then was to pluck the fatal rose from the pommel and hand it to Beauty, saying, "Here is what you asked me to bring. You little know what it will cost you all."

This, and his sorrowful look, gave the eldest daughter her cue. "I was certain of it!" she said. "Did I not say, all along, that to force a rose at this time of the year would cost you more than to have bought presents for all the rest of us? A rose, in midwinter! And such a rose! There—one has only to look at it to see that you took good care Beauty should have her present, no matter at what cost to us!"

"It is all too true," answered their father sorrowfully, "that this rose has cost me dear—far dearer than all the presents you others begged of me. But the cost is not in money, for would to God I could have bought it with the last penny in my purse!"

His speech excited their curiosity, and they

gave him no rest until he had told the whole of his story. It left their hopes utterly dashed. The daughters lamented their loss, while their brothers hardily declared that they would never allow their father to return to this accursed castle—they would march there together and destroy the horrible beast who owned it. But their father assured them that he had given his word and would rather die than break it.

The sisters then turned upon Beauty and started to upbraid and rail against her.

"It is all your fault," they declared. "This is what comes of your pretended modesty! Why could you not have asked for dresses and jewels as we did? Even if you could not get them, at least the demand would have cost nothing. But you chose to be different—you, with your precious rose! And now our father must die, and we must all suffer because of your affectation!"

Poor Beauty controlled her tears and replied, "Yes, I am to blame for all this, though, indeed, dear sisters, I did it innocently. For how could I guess that to ask for a rose in the middle of summer, as it was then, would give rise to all this misery? But what does that matter? Innocent or guilty, I cannot allow you to suffer for what was my fault. And so I will go back with our father to save him from his promise. That will be in a month's time, and in this little month, I beg of you, let us be happy together without reproaches."

At first her brothers would not hear of any such sacrifice, and her father was equally set against it, until the sisters, again fired up in their jealousy, accused him of being distressed only because it happened to be Beauty. If another of his daughters, they hinted, had offered to pay this price for his life, he would have accepted it cheerfully enough!

Beauty ended this talk by saying firmly that, whether they wished it or not, she would go. "And who knows," she said, forcing a brave smile, "but this fate of mine, which seems so terrible, may cover some extraordinary and happy fortune." She said it merely to hearten them, but her sisters, fancying her deluded by vanity and self-conceit, smiled maliciously and applauded.

So their father gave way, and it was agreed that Beauty must go. For her part, she desired only that the few days remaining to her might be as happy as possible. And so, as the days passed she spoke little of what was before her, and, if at all, only to treat it lightly and as a piece of good fortune.

*W*hen the time drew near Beauty shared all all her trinkets and little possessions with her sisters—for, as badly as they had treated her, they were the only friends she had. Yet jealousy had made their hearts so wicked that when the fatal day arrived they actually rejoiced to hear the neighing of a horse which, punctually sent by the beast, arrived at the door of the cottage.

The brothers would have rushed out and slain the beautiful animal, but Beauty, overcoming their anger with a few tender words, bade her father mount into the saddle. And bidding her sisters farewell with a tenderness that forced them to weep at the last, she climbed to the pillion behind him quite as if she were setting out for a holiday.

They were off! The horse seemed to fly rather than to gallop and so smoothly that Beauty could scarcely feel the motion save by the soft wind that beat on her cheek. Soon they caught sight of the castle in the distance. Her father, less happy than she, again and again asked and begged her to alight and return. It was a most idle offer, for he had no

real control of the reins. But Beauty did not listen, because her mind was made up.

Nevertheless, she was awed, and all the more when, as the fleet horse galloped up to the courtyard, they were met by a great salvo of guns and, as the echoes died away, by the sound of soft music within the palace.

The horse had come to a stop next to a flight of agate steps. A light shone down these steps from a porchway, within which the violins kept their throbbing. Beauty slipped down from the saddle, and her father, alighting after her, took her by the hand and led her to the chamber in which he had first supped. There, sure enough, they found a cheerful fire and a score of candles lit and burning with an exquisite perfume, and—best of all—a table laid with the daintiest of suppers.

The merchant, accustomed to the ways of their host, knew that the supper was meant for them, and Beauty began to eat with a good appetite. Her spirits indeed were rising. There had been no sign of any beast in all the many rooms through which she had passed, and everything in them had seemed to breathe of gaiety and good living.

But this happy frame of mind did not last long. They had scarcely finished supper when the beast was heard coming through the distant rooms. At the sound—the heavy padding of his feet, the roar of his breath—Beauty clung to her father in terror, and had almost fainted against the arm which he flung around her. But when the beast stood before her in the doorway, after a little shudder she walked toward him with a firm step, and, halting at a little distance, saluted him respectfully. This behavior evidently pleased the beast. After letting his eyes rest on her face for a while, he said, in a tone that might well have struck terror into the boldest heart (and yet it did not seem to be angry), "Good evening, my good sir! Good evening, Beauty!"

The merchant was far too terrified to find his voice, but Beauty controlled hers and answered sweetly, "Good evening, Beast!"

"Have you come here of your own free will?" asked the beast. "And are you willing to let your father return and leave you here?"

Beauty answered that she was quite willing.

"Indeed?" And yet what do you suppose will happen to you after he has gone?"

"Sir," said Beauty, "that is as it pleases you, and you only can tell."

"Well answered," replied the beast, "and since you have come of your own accord, you shall stay. As for you, my good sir," said he to the merchant, "you will take your departure at sunrise. The bell will give you warning. Delay not to rise, eat your breakfast, and depart as before. But remember that you are forbidden ever to come within sight of my palace again."

Then, turning to Beauty, he said, "Take your father into the next room, and choose between you everything you think will please your brothers and sisters. You will find there two traveling trunks. Fill them as full as they will hold."

Sorrowful as she was at the certainty of losing her father so soon and forever, Beauty made ready to obey the beast's orders, and he left them as he had come, saying, "Good night, Beauty! Good night, good sir!"

When they were alone, Beauty and her father went into the next room, which proved to be a storeroom piled with treasures a king and queen might have envied. After choosing and setting apart in heaps—one for each of her sisters—the most magnificent dresses she could find, Beauty opened a cupboard which had a door of crystal framed in gold, and stood for a moment dazzled by the precious stones that lay piled on every shelf. After choosing a vast number and adding them to her heaps, she opened yet another wardrobe and found it full of money in gold pieces. This set her pondering.

"I think, Father," she said, "that we had better empty these trunks again, and fill them with money. For money can always be turned to account, whereas to sell these precious stones you would have to go to some jeweler, who very likely would cheat you, and perhaps be suspicious of them. But with these pieces of gold you can buy land, houses, furniture, jewels—what you will—and no one will ask any questions."

Her father agreed. Yet he first tried to make room for the money by emptying out the few things he had packed for himself. But this was no good, for it seemed that the trunks were made in folds which opened the wider the more he put in. Somehow the more they packed, the more room there seemed to be, and they ended by replacing all the dresses and precious stones they had taken out. But now the trunks were so heavy that an elephant would have sunk under them.

"It is all a cheat!" cried the merchant. "The beast is mocking us, and only pretended to give us these things, knowing that I could not carry them away."

"Wait a little," advised Beauty. "That would be a sorry jest, and I cannot help thinking that the beast is honest, and that since he offered these gifts he will find you also the means to carry them. The best thing we can do is to strap up the trunks and leave them ready here."

So they did this and went back to the little room, where, to their amazement, they found a breakfast laid on the table. For a moment they could scarcely believe that the night had flown by while they were occupied in ransacking the treasure chamber and packing the trunks. But, glancing at the windows, they saw that day was indeed breaking. Presently a bell sounded, warning the merchant to eat quickly and depart.

He finished his meal, and they went down together to the courtyard, where two horses stood ready—the one laden with the trunks, the other saddled for the merchant to ride. And now Beauty and her father would have spent a long time in bidding one another farewell. But the two horses neighed and pawed the ground so impatiently that he was afraid to linger. Tearing himself from his daughter's arms he mounted in haste, and could scarcely turn to say good-bye before both horses sprang away swift as the wind and he was lost to sight in an instant.

Poor Beauty! She gazed and gazed through her tears, and so mounted the stairs sorrowfully back to her own chamber. On reaching it she felt herself oppressed with sleepiness, for she had passed the night without undressing, and, moreover, for a month past her sleep had been broken and haunted with terrors. So, having nothing better to do, she went to bed, and was nestling down in the perfumed sheets when her eyes fell on the little table by the bedside. Someone had set a cup of hot chocolate there, and half asleep, she reached out her hand for it and drank it. Immediately her eyes closed and she fell into a delicious slumber, such as she had not known since the day when her father brought home the fatal rose.

She dreamed that she was walking alongside an endless canal, the banks of which were bordered with tall orange trees and myrtles in flower. There, as she wandered disconsolately lamenting her fate, all of a sudden a young prince stood before her. He was handsome as the God of Love in picture books, and when he spoke it was with a voice that went straight to her heart.

"Dear Beauty," he said, "you are not so unfortunate as you suppose. It is here you shall find the reward of your goodness, denied to you elsewhere. Use your wits to find me out under the disguise which hides me—that is, if as I stand here now you find me not altogether contemptible. For I love you tenderly—you alone—and in making me happy you can attain your own happiness. Beloved, never distrust your own true heart, and it shall lead you where the heart has nothing left to desire." So saying, the charming apparition knelt at her feet, and again besought her to accept his devotion and become mistress over all his life.

"Ah! What can I do to make you happy?" she asked earnestly.

"Only be grateful," he answered, "and do not believe all that your eyes would tell you. Above all, do not abandon me until you have rescued me from the cruel sufferings I endure."

With that the dream melted away, but only to be succeeded by another. She found herself face to face with a stately and beautiful lady. The lady was speaking to her with dignity, yet most kindly.

"Dear Beauty," she said, "do not grieve for what you have left behind. A far higher destiny lies before you. Only, if you would deserve it, beware of being misled by appearances."

Beauty found her dreams so agreeable that she was in no hurry at all to awake, and even when her eyes opened to the daylight she had more than half a mind to close them again. But a clock, chiming out her own name twelve times, warned her that it was midday and time to get up. She rose, therefore, and found her dressing table set out with brushes and combs and everything she could want. After she had dressed carefully, and with a lightness of heart for which she found it hard to account, she passed into the next room and found her dinner on the table.

Dinner does not take very long when you are

all by yourself. Beauty, when she had eaten enough, sat down on a sofa and began to think of the handsome youth she had seen in her dream. He told me I could make him happy, she thought. Why, then, it must be that the horrible beast, who appears to be master here, is keeping him a prisoner. How can I set him free? They both warned me not to trust to appearances. It is all very puzzling. . . . But one thing is clear at any rate, that I am very silly to be vexing my head over a dream. I will forget all about it, and look for something to do to amuse myself.

She sprang up, and started to make a tour of discovery through the many rooms of the palace. They were even grander than she had expected. The first she entered was lined with mirrors from floor to ceiling, where she saw herself reflected on every side. The next thing to catch her eye was a bracelet, hanging from one of the chandeliers. Set in the bracelet was a gold locket. Opening this she was startled indeed, for it contained a portrait in miniature of the gallant youth she had seen in her dream. She could not be mistaken, so closely were his features engraved on her memory— yes, and, it may be, on her heart. She slipped the bracelet on her wrist, without stopping to think that it did not belong to her, and went on to explore further. She passed into a long picture gallery, and there again she met the prince's face. It smiled down at her, this time from a life-sized portrait, and it seemed to smile so wistfully that she caught herself blushing.

From the gallery her steps had led her to a chamber filled with instruments of music. Beauty was an accomplished musician. So, sitting down, she amused herself by tuning and trying one instrument after another, but she liked the harp best because that went best with her voice.

Leaving the music room at length, she found herself in a long chamber like the picture gallery, but lined with books. It held an immense library. Beauty, ever since she had lived in the country, had been forced to do without reading, for her father had sold all his books to pay his debts. Now, as her eyes traveled along the shelves, she knew she need never have any fear that time would pass heavily here. The dusk was gathering before she had half-studied even the titles of the thousands of volumes. And numbers of candles, waxen and scented, in chandeliers with lusters of diamonds and rubies, were beginning to light themselves in every room.

In due time, Beauty found supper laid and served for her, with the same good taste and orderliness as before, and still she had seen no living face. What did this matter? Her father had warned her that she would be alone. And she was beginning to tell herself that she could be alone here without much discomfort, when she heard the noise of the beast approaching. She could not help trembling a little, for she had not yet found herself alone with him, and knew not what would happen. He might even be coming to devour her. But when he appeared he did not seem at all ferocious.

"Good evening, Beauty," he said gruffly.

"Good evening, Beast," she answered gently, but shaking a little.

"Do you think you can be content here?" he asked.

Beauty answered politely that it ought not to be hard to live happily in such a beautiful palace.

After this they talked for an hour, and in the course of their talk Beauty began to excuse many things in the beast—his voice, for example. With such a nose how could he help roaring through it? Really, he appeared to be wanting in tact rather than purposely terrible, although, to be sure, this want of tact terrified her cruelly, when at length he blurted out, "Will you be my wife, Beauty?"

Ah! I am lost! thought Beauty. The beast could not be so dull-witted after all, for, although she kept the cry to herself, he answered quickly, and just as if she had uttered it aloud, "Not at all. I wish you to answer just 'yes' or 'no.' "

"Oh! No, Beast."

"Very well, then," said this tractable monster. "Since you will not, I had best be going. Good night, Beauty."

"Good night, Beast," answered Beauty, relieved

of her fright. She felt sure now that he did not mean to hurt her, and as soon as he had taken his leave she went off to bed, and was asleep in no time.

But almost as quickly she was dreaming. And in her dream at once she saw her unknown lover standing beside her, handsome as ever, but more sorrowful than before.

"Dear Beauty," he said, "why are you so cruel to me? I love you the better for being so stubborn, and yet it lengthens my misery."

She could not understand this at all. Her dream wavered and it seemed to her that he took a hundred different shapes in it. Now he had a crown between his hands and was offering it to her. Now he was kneeling at her feet. Now he smiled, radiant with joy. And again he buried his head in despair and wept until the sound of his sobbing pieced her heart. Thus, in one aspect or another, he was with her the night through.

She awoke with him in her thoughts, and her first act was to unclasp the locket on her wrist and assure herself that the miniature was like him. It certainly was the same face, and his, too, was the face that smiled down from the larger portrait in the gallery. But the face in the locket gave her a more secret joy and she unclasped the miniature and gazed at it again and again.

*O*ne morning she went down into the gardens, where the sun shone inviting her to ramble. They were lovely beyond imagination. Here stood a statue showered over with roses. There fountain on fountain played and threw a refreshing spray so high in the air that her eyes could scarcely reach to its summit. But what most surprised her was that every nook and corner recalled those she had seen in her dreams with the unknown prince standing beside her.

At length she came to the long canal with the oranges and myrtles in the shade of which she had first seen him approach. It was the very spot, and she could no longer disbelieve that her dreams were real. She felt sure, now, that he must somehow be imprisoned here, and resolved to get at the truth that very evening, should the beast repeat his visit.

Tired at last of wandering, she returned to the palace and discovered a new room full of materials for work to engage the most idle—tape bags, looms, silks for embroidery, scissors, and thimbles. Beyond this needlework room a door opened upon the most wonderful sight of all—an aviary full of the rarest birds, yet all so tame that they flew to Beauty, and perched themselves on her shoulders.

"Dear birds," she said, "I wish you were closer to my own room, that I might sit and hear you singing."

She had scarcely said it when, opening a door beyond the aviary, she found herself in her own chamber—yes, her very own!—which she had thought to be quite on the other side of the building. The door, when she came to examine it, had a shutter which could be opened to hear, and closed again when she grew tired of it. This aviary opened on another inhabited by parrots, parakeets, and cockatoos. These no sooner saw Beauty than they began to scream and chatter. One wished her "Good morning," another invited her to luncheon, while a third yet more gallant cried "Kiss me! Kiss me!" Others whistled airs from grand opera or declaimed pieces of poetry by the best authors. It was plain that in their several ways they all had the same object—to amuse her.

Beyond the aviaries lay a monkey house. Here were apes of all sorts—Barbary apes, mandarin apes, apes with blue faces, baboons, marmosets, chimpanzees—and all came frisking about her, bowing and scraping, to show how much they appreciated the honor of this visit. To celebrate it

they stretched a tightrope and danced, and threw somersaults with an agility which Beauty found highly diverting. And yet she could not help sighing that none of these animals were able to tell her news of her unknown prince. She patted and made much of them, however, and asked if some of them would be kind enough to come with her and keep her company.

At once, and as if they had only been waiting for this command, two large female apes in sweeping court dresses stepped to her side and became her maids of honor. Two brisk little marmosets volunteered for pages and held up her train, while an affable baboon, his face wreathed with smiles, bowed, presented a gloved hand, and begged leave to squire her. With this singular escort, Beauty marched back to luncheon. And while she ate it the birds piped and fluted around her for accompaniment to the parrots, who lifted up their voices and chanted the latest and most fashionable tunes. The meal was no sooner ended than the apes begged her to allow them to entertain her with a light comedy, which (leave being granted) they proceeded to act in a highly credible manner and with appropriate mime, while the parrots spoke the words from the wings very distinctly and in accents that exactly conformed with the various parts. At the close, one of the actors advanced, laid his hand on his heart and—still with the parrot for interpreter—thanked

Beauty for the indulgence she had shown to their poor efforts.

That night again, after supper, the beast paid her his accustomed visit. He put the same questions, and received her answers as before. And, as before, the conversation ended by his taking leave of her with a "Good night, Beauty." The two female apes, as ladies-in-waiting, thereupon undressed their mistress and saw her to bed. Before leaving, they thoughtfully opened the window shutter, that the soft night-warbling of the birds might soothe her to sleep and dream of her lover.

*I*n this fashion day followed day, and still Beauty found plenty to amuse her. At the end of a week she made the most wonderful discovery of all. There was one large room which she had entered only once, because it seemed to her rather dull and dark, too. It was empty, and although it had four windows in each wall, only two of them admitted any light. One day, as she passed the door, the fancy took her to open one of these windows. She stepped in and drew the shutter, when to her astonishment it opened, not upon daylight after all, but what seemed to be a dim hall lit only by a glimmer, distant and faint, behind the chinks of a thick curtain at the far end. She was wondering what this might mean, when the curtain went up and in a sudden flood of light she found herself gazing, as from a box, into a theater crowded from floor to ceiling, and with an audience brilliant in dresses and jewels.

An orchestra played the overture, and gave place to the actors—real actors this time, not apes and parrots. The play was charming, and Beauty was in ecstasy with every scene of it. When the curtain fell she lingered in her box, hoping to see the fashionable crowd disperse. But somewhat to her chagrin the lights went out almost at once and the theater was dark again. Still it had been very pleasant, and she promised herself to become a constant playgoer.

That evening when the beast paid his visit, she told him all about the comedy. "Eh? You like that sort of thing, do you?" asked the monster. "Well, you shall have as much of it as you like. You are so pretty." Beauty could not help smiling inwardly at his clumsy compliments. But she smiled no longer when he put to her once again his blunt question: "Beauty, will you be my wife?"

"No, Beast," she answered as before, but she was really beginning to get frightened, he was so gentle and so persistent. She sat up so long thinking about this that it was almost daylight before she closed her eyes in bed. And at once, as if impatient at being kept waiting, the lover of her dreams presented himself. Perhaps for this reason he was not in the best of tempers. At any rate he accused her of being moody and discontented.

"I should be happy enough," she answered, "if the beast did not pester me so. I—I almost think, by his foolish compliments, that he would like me to marry him." Beauty expected her dream-lover to show some jealousy at this, but seeing that he merely stood glum, she went on, "Would you really be content if I married him? But alas! No. Were he as charming as he is hideous, you know that I love you and can never love anyone else."

By all rights the prince should have been in raptures at this avowal, but his answer was, "Dearest, love him who best loves you. Do not be led astray by appearances, and so you will free me from captivity."

This was not only puzzling, it also seemed to Beauty to be just a little selfish. "At least," she said, "tell me what to do. Since liberty appears to be your first wish, believe me, I would liberate you at any sacrifice, if only I knew how." But this was what she could never discover, and because of it her nights now, though she longed for them, troubled her more than her days.

Her days passed pleasantly enough, and still in fresh discoveries. One by one in their turn she opened the windows of the great hall, and they revealed many delights.

First, there was a grand performance of opera. And she listened not only to the singers, but also to the murmur of the audience between the acts. To listen to this and to gaze on human faces, gave her inexpressible pleasure.

Next, there was a great fair in progress. When first she looked the throng had not arrived and she leisurely inspected the booths with their various wares. As the spectators drifted in, the drums began to beat, the hobby horses to revolve, the showmen to shout, and the marionettes to perform in their little theater. It was ravishing.

After this she beheld a fashionable promenade, with a richly dressed crowd passing to and fro, exchanging greetings, remarking how superb was the weather, and pausing to admire and criticize the shop windows to the right and left.

The next spectacle was a gaming room, with the players seated at their cards or roulette, the croupiers spinning the ball or raking the money. Beauty, with nothing to stake, had leisure to observe their faces, and how sadly some left the tables who had come smiling with money in their pockets. She saw, too, that some were being cheated, and it vexed her because she could not warn them.

Next, she was gazing at the Royal Palace, where the King and Queen were holding a reception. She saw ambassadors with their wives, lords and ladies and state counselors, and watched them as they passed by the throne making their lowest bows.

A water picnic followed this. The boats lay moored alongside a bank where the merrymakers sat or lounged and talked to the sound of lutes. The picnic ended in a ball, with violins playing and couples advancing and retreating on the waxed floor that shone in the light of a thousand candles. Oh, how Beauty longed to be one of the dancers!

But perhaps the last window gave her the most pleasure. For through it she was able to see the whole world at one gaze and all that was going on in it. State embassies, royal weddings, coronations, pageants, armies, revolutions, sieges, pitched battles—she could sit at her ease and watch them all, which was far more amusing than it is to read about them in a newspaper.

She ought, you will say, to have been happy as the day was long. But no. A life becomes flat and stale which is a perpetual round of pleasure and leaves nothing to sigh or to hope for. Beauty began to long for a sight of her father and her brothers and sisters. She concealed this for a while, however, and turned her thoughts to what was more pressing. For she could not beg leave to go home until something had been done to rescue her dear prince and restore him to liberty. The beast alone, she reflected, could tell her the secret. And she thought to herself that, being himself so blunt of speech, he would forgive some bluntness in her. So one evening she asked him point blank, "Beast, are we alone in this palace, with nobody but ourselves?"

"Of course we are," he answered gruffly, but the question appeared in some way to sting him, for almost at once he rose and bade her good night.

Now Beauty, whatever else she thought of the beast, had by this time learned to trust him to be honest. It was a dreadful disappointment, therefore, to be forced to believe on his word that her prince had no existence outside of her fancy. She slept badly that night. In her dream she was wandering again and sorrowfully alongside the canal when her lover appeared and took her hands between his while he scanned her face, which was bathed in tears.

"What has gone wrong, dear Beauty?" he demanded. "Why are you in this distress? Ah, it is the beast who persecutes you! But, never fear, you shall be delivered here and now from his attention." And with these words the prince snatched out a dagger and rushed on the monster, who now for the first time came into the dream, advancing slowly down the bank of the canal. Strange to say, he offered no resistance even when the dagger almost touched his throat. But Beauty, whom an unseen power held back as she would have run to prevent the murder, on the instant found voice to cry, "Stay! Stay, rash fool! Kill me before you kill him who has been my best friend!"

"Friend?" answered the prince, still with his dagger lifted. "And am I no more than that?"

"You are an unfaithful friend, at any rate," persisted Beauty, "if, knowing well that I would lay down my life for you, you would take the life of one who has done me so much kindness." But while she pleaded the figures wavered in her dream, still struggling together, and vanished, giving place to the same stately lady she had seen in her former vision.

"Courage, Beauty!" said this new phantom, "your happiness is not far off, if only you will go your own way and trust not to appearances."

This dream left Beauty so uneasy that the next day she opened one window after another to cure her restlessness. And when this would not do, she opened all the windows together, but still in vain.

That night, when the beast paid his usual visit, he detected almost at once that she had been weeping, and demanded to know the reason.

"Ah, sir," said Beauty, "if only I might go home!"

"You wish to go home?" The beast's face

turned pale—which, for such a face, was no easy matter. He staggered backward with a deep sigh, or rather, a roar of grief. "Ah, Beauty, Beauty! Would you desert a poor beast? What more can I do to make you happy? Or is it because you hate me, that you wish to be gone?"

"No, Beast," answered Beauty gently, "I do not hate you, and I should be very sorry never to see you again. But I do long to see my own people. Let me go home for two months only, and I promise to come back and stay with you for the rest of my life."

The beast had fallen flat and lay along the carpet at her feet. His eyes were closed, and for some while his heavy sighs alone told her that he was neither dead nor in a swoon. By and by he lifted his head. "I can deny you nothing," he said sadly. "But no matter, though it cost me my life. . . . In the room next to your bedroom you will find four chests. Fill them with everything you would like to take with you. Be sure to keep your word, for if you break it and come back to find your poor Beast dead, you will be sorry then when it is too late. Come back at the end of two months and you will find me alive. And to come back you will not need a chariot or horses. Only say good-bye, that night, to your father, and brothers, and sisters. And, when you are in bed, turn this ring around on your finger and say firmly, 'I wish to go back to my palace and see my Beast again.' That is all. Good night, Beauty! Sleep soundly, and in good time you shall see your father once more."

*A*s soon as he was gone, Beauty set to work to fill the four boxes with all the riches and finery that her heart could desire. She filled them to the brim, and then, tired out, she went to bed. But for a long while she could not close her eyes for excitement. It was not until almost sunrise that sleep visited her and, with it, another dream. In this dream she saw her beloved prince stretched at full length on a bank of turf. His face was hidden, and she could hear that he was sobbing. But when, touched by the sight of his grief, she drew near to console him, he lifted his face to her and said, "Cruel Beauty, how can you ask what ails me? When you are leaving me, and your going is my death warrant!"

"But, dearest Prince," said Beauty, "I am only going to tell my father and brothers and sisters that I am well and happy. In a short while I shall be back, never to leave you again. But, for that matter," she went on as a new thought struck her, "why should we be separated at all? I will put off my going for another day, and tomorrow I will beg the beast to let you go with me. I am sure he will not refuse."

"I can only go with you, if you promise me never to come back," replied the prince. "And, after all, when you have once delivered me, why should we ever come back? The beast will be hurt in his feelings and very angry no doubt, but by that time we shall be beyond his power."

"You forget," Beauty reminded him sharply, "that I have promised him to return, and that, moreover, he says he will die of grief if I break my word."

"And what if he does?" demanded her lover. "Is not your happiness worth more than the life of a monster? Of what use is he in the world except to frighten folks out of their wits?"

"Ah, you do not understand!" cried Beauty. "This monster— as you call him—is only a monster in his face, and through no fault of his. He has the kindest heart in the world, and how could I be so ungrateful after all he has done for me!"

"I believe," said her lover bitterly, "that if you saw us fighting, of the two you would rather let me perish than this beast of yours."

Beauty told him that he was cruel and unjust, and begged him to talk of something else. She set the example, too. Seeing that he was piqued and proud, she addressed a long speech to him, full of endearments, to win him back to a good humor, and was growing astonished at her own eloquence when, in the middle of it, she awoke.

Her last words seemed to mingle with the sound of familiar voices. She sprang out of bed and drew her curtain. It was very strange! As the sunlight poured in she saw that she was in a room much more poorly furnished than that in which she had fallen asleep. She dressed in haste and, opening the door, found that the next room, too, was like no apartment in the beast's palace. But at her feet stood the four chests she had packed overnight. And, while she marveled, again she heard a voice talking, and ran toward it. For it was her father's.

She rushed out and fell into his arms. He, poor man, stared at her as though she had sprung from another world, and the others were no less astonished. Her brothers embraced her with transports of joy, while her sisters—who, to tell the truth, had not overcome their jealousy—pretended to be quite as glad. They plied her with a thousand questions, which she answered very good-naturedly, putting aside her own impatience, for she, too, had a number of questions to ask. To begin with, this house of theirs was not the cottage in which she had left them, but a fine new one her father had been able to buy with the beast's presents. If not wealthy, he was in easy circumstances. With the bettering of their fortunes his sisters had found other wooers and were soon to be married. And altogether Beauty had the satisfaction of knowing that she had at least brought prosperity back to her family.

"As for you, my dearest child," said the merchant, "when your sisters are married, you shall keep house for your brothers and me, and so my old age will be happy."

This was all very well, but Beauty had to tell her father that she must leave him again in two months time, whereupon he broke out into lamentations.

"Dear Father," said the sensible girl, "it is good of you to weep, but it is useless, and I would rather have your advice, which is sure to be useful." Thereupon she told him all the story.

Her father considered for a while, and then said, "I can only give you the same counsel that, by your own admission, you are always receiving from these phantoms of your dreams. 'Do not trust to appearance,' they say, and 'Be guided by your heart's gratitude,' and they tell you this over and over again. What can it mean, child, but one thing? The beast, you say, is frightful. His appearance is certainly against him. Then judge him rather by the gratitude which you certainly owe him. It is plain that he has a good heart—'handsome is as handsome does'—it is clear to me that these phantoms would have you say 'Yes' to the beast, and I, too, advise you to consent."

Beauty saw the wisdom of this and knew very well that her father was counseling her for the best. Nevertheless, it needed something more than this to reconcile her with marrying a monster, and she felt relieved at the thought that for two whole months she could put off deciding.

Strange to say, as the days went by and the time of her departure drew nearer, she found herself looking forward to it rather than repining. For one thing distressed her and spoiled all her happiness—she never dreamed at all now.

The days went by, and as they drew to an end her brothers and even her father (forgetting his former good counsel) employed all persuasions to hinder her departure. But her mind was made up. And when the two months were passed she was resolute on everything but the hour of her parting. Every morning, when she got up, she meant to say good-bye, but somehow another night came and the farewells were still unspoken.

She reproached herself (as well she might), and was still thus cruelly torn between two minds, when one night a dream visited her—the first for two months and more.

She dreamed that she was back at the beast's palace, and wandering by a lonely path in the gardens which ended in a tangle of brushwood overhanging a cave. As she drew nearer she heard a terrible groaning, and running in haste she found the beast stretched there on the point of death. Still in her dream she was bending over him when the stately lady stepped forth from the bushes and addressed her in a tone of grave reproach, "I doubt, Beauty, if even now you have come in time. Cruel, cruel of you to delay, when your delay has brought him so near to death!"

Terrified by this dream, Beauty awoke in her bed with a start. "I have done wickedly!" she cried. "Am I too late? Oh, indeed I hope not!" She turned the ring upon her finger and said aloud in a firm voice, "I wish to go back to my palace and see my Beast again!"

With that she at once fell asleep, and only woke up to hear the clock chiming, "Beauty, Beauty," twelve times on the musical note she so well remembered. She was back, then, at the palace. Yes, and—oh, joy!—her faithful apes and parrots were gathered around the bed, wishing her good morning!

But none of them could tell her any news of the beast. They were here to serve her, and all their thoughts ended with their duty. Their good master—the lord of this splendid palace—what was he to them? At any rate nothing was to be learned from them, and Beauty was no sooner dressed than she broke away impatiently, wandering through the house and the gardens to fill up the time until evening should bring his accustomed visit. But it was hard work filling up the time. She went into the great hall and resolutely opened the windows one by one. The shows were there as before, but opera and comedy, fete and pageant, held no meaning for her. The players were listless, the music was dull, the processions passed before her eyes but had lost their power to amuse.

Supper time came at last. But when after supper the minutes passed and passed and still no beast appeared, then indeed Beauty was frightened. For a long time she waited, listened, told herself this and that, and finally in a terror rushed down into the gardens to seek for him. The alleys were dark. The bushes daunted her with their black shadows. But still up and down ran poor Beauty, calling to the beast, and calling in vain.

She was drenched with the dew, utterly lost and weary, when, after three hours, pausing for a moment's rest, she saw before her the same solitary path she had seen in her dream. And there in the moonlight she almost stumbled over the beast.

He lay there, stretched at full length and asleep—or so she thought. So glad was she to have found him that she knelt and stroked his head, calling him by name over and over. But his flesh was cold beneath her hand, nor did he move or open his eyes.

"Ah, he is dead!" she cried, aghast.

But she put a hand over his heart, and to her inexpressible joy she felt that it was still beating. Hastily she ran to a fountain nearby, and dipping water into her palms from its basin she ran and sprinkled it on his face, coaxing him with tender words as his eyes opened, and slowly—very slowly— he came to himself.

"Ah! what a fright you have given me!" she murmured. "Dear Beast, I never knew how I loved you until I feared that you were dead—yes, dead, and through my fault! But I believe, if you had died, I should have died, too."

"Beauty," said the beast faintly, "you are very good if indeed you can love such an ugly brute as I am. It is true that I was dying for you, and should have died if you had not come. I thought you had forsaken me. But are you sure?"

"Sure of what?" asked Beauty.

"That you love me?"

"Let us go back to supper," said Beauty, raising his head.

"Yes, let us go back to supper," agreed the beast, lifting himself heavily on her arm. He still leaned on her, as they walked back to the palace together. But the supper—which they found laid for two—seemed to revive him, and in his old stupid way he asked her about the time she had spent at home, and if her father and brothers and sisters had been glad to see her.

Beauty, though weary enough after her search through the park and gardens, stirred herself to tell him about everything that had happened to her while she was away. The beast sat nodding his head and listening in his old dull way—which somehow seemed to her the most comfortable way in the world. At length he rose to go. But at the doorway he put the old blunt question:

"Beauty, will you marry me?"

"Yes, dear Beast," said Beauty. And as she said it a blaze of light filled the room. A salvo of artillery sounded, a moment later, from the park. Bang, bang! Fireworks shot across the windows of the palace. Sky rockets and Roman candles exploded and across the darkness in letters of fire were written the words LONG LIVE BEAUTY AND THE BEAST!

Beauty turned to ask what all these rejoicings might mean. And with that, she gave a cry. The beast had vanished, and in his place stood the beloved prince of her dreams! He smiled and stretched out his hands to her. Scarcely knowing what she did, she was stretching out hers to take them, when above the banging of fireworks in the avenues there sounded a rolling of wheels. It drew to the porch, and presently there entered the stately lady she had seen in her dreams. It was the very same, and, astounded as she was, Beauty curtseyed to her.

But the stately lady was just as eager to curtsey to Beauty. "Best and dearest," said she, "my son is going to love you always. How should he not, seeing that by your courage you have rescued him from the enchantment under which he has lain so long, and have restored him to his natural form? But suffer also his mother, a Queen, to bless you!"

Beauty turned again to her lover and saw that he, who had been a beast, was indeed the prince of her dreams and handsomer than the day. So they were married and lived happily ever after. Nay, so happy were they that all over the world folks told one another and set down in writing this wonderful history of Beauty and the Beast.

Maidens, from this tale of Beauty
    Learn, and in your memory write—
Daily leads a Path of Duty
    Through the Garden of Delight;
Where the loveliest roses wear
    Daunting thorns, for you to dare.